Cindyrella

A Musical for Young People

Written by Therese Marlin

Original Music by Elaine Friedlander

Baker's Plays
7611 Sunset Blvd.
Los Angeles, CA 90046
bakersplays.com

CINDYRELLA was produced twice in 2000 by Dr. Jonathan Ogbonna, Principal and Ms. Laura Puma, Music Teacher with eighth grade students at Yorkship Family School, Camden, NJ for the student body and its parents. In 2001, it was produced by Urban Promise, a summer program for inner city high school students, for the community at large.

CHARACTERS

CINDYRELLA – an orphan cousin from the South

LAVINIA KRUALL – aunt and caretaker of Cindyrella

PENELOPE KRUALL – daughter of Lavinia, walks strangely, high pitched voice

ADRIENNE KRUALL – second daughter of Lavinia, sneezes and blows her nose a lot

MRS. ZEBALON – an old woman full of wisdom and strange ways, neighbor

MR. GILL – neighbor on the other side, Uncle of Arsinio Charming

ARSINIO CHARMING – (Junior) talent scout for Prince Records

ASSISTANT I – helper of Arsinio

ASSISTANT 2 – helper of Arsinio

NARRATOR

Assorted acts trying out for talent search

AUTHOR'S NOTE

Young people of all ethnic groups can identify with the courage and resilience in dealing with the shift in the family configuration and with Cindyrella's reliance on and appreciation of community support. CINDYRELLA is a musical play to be performed either by: young people between the ages of 10-14, or young adults for children of all ages. The original music, based on American music genre influenced by African and Caribbean rhythms, is designed to appeal to and to be performed by young people. The running time of the production is between 40-60 minutes. There are 10 speaking parts. The number of drummers and of dancers is optional, as is the use of a chorus.

SCENES

ACT I

Scene 1 – Kruall House Interior, *weekend morning*

Scene 2 – Kruall House Interior (Breakfast), *a week later*

Scene 3 – Backyards, *later that day*

Scene 4 – Kruall House Interior, *a few days later, on Saturday*

ACT II

Scene 1 – Zebalon 's House, *later that day*

Scene 2 – Talent Contest Stage, *later that day (Saturday)*

Scene 3 – Kruall House Interior, *later that day*

ACT I

Scene 1

NARRATOR. Cinderella is a very old fairy tale repeated in various ways by many different cultures. It has been made into an Italian opera, a Russian ballet and a Disney movie. Tonight *(Today)* we will present another version that just might have taken place in *(Local town/city.)*. We hope that you enjoy it.

(Home of the Krualls, living room and kitchen visible, couch, chairs,
  table chairs, TV, kitchen appliances, telephone — living room
  stage right; kitchen stage left.
When the scene opens, LAVINIA is looking through the want ads.
  She keeps moving the paper in and out and squinting to see
  each ad. She circles this one and that one, shaking her head at
  others. PENELOPE is on the telephone and ADRIENNE is
  doing her nails singing off key to herself.)

PENELOPE. *(Talking into the phone.)* What? Talent search right here in *(Our town/city.)*? No, girl. *(Pause)* For real? Of course I'm gonna' get a registration form!

LAVINIA. Penelope, get off that phone. You've got homework to do. And you stop that screeching, Adrienne. I can't concentrate on these want ads.

PENELOPE. *(Into phone.)* 'Got to go. 'By.

ADRIENNE. *(Sighs)* Yes, Momma.

PENELOPE. Momma, you're never gonna' believe this. Prince Records is having a talent search right here in *(Our town.)*.

7

LAVINIA. *(Moving the paper closer, then further away.)* Did I miss something? I don't see any talent search in the want ads.

PENELOPE. *(Jumping up and down.)* Momma, I'm gonna' get a registration form!

ADRIENNE. *(Snatching the paper.)* Here it is, Momma. *(Reads)* Boys and girls between the ages of 12 and 17 may pick up a registration form to aud-audition for Prince Records on *(Select a date. Puts paper down.)* Momma you gotta' pick me up a registration form.

PENELOPE. ...and one for me, too. *(Knock on door, stage right.)* I'll get it. *(She walks across the floor waving her arms and walking with her feet turned out. She opens the door.)* Who are you?

CINDYRELLA. Is this the home of Mrs. Lavinia Kruall?

PENELOPE. Who wants to know?

LAVINIA. *(Rising from the chair.)* Close that door. I'm not about to heat the whole street. *(Approaching the girl who has entered.)* Who are you?

CINDYRELLA. Aunt Lavinia! *(She puts down her suitcase and rushes over to hug LAVINIA.)*

LAVINIA. Get this girl off me! I never saw her before in my life.

(PENELOPE and ADRIENNE awkwardly try to remove CINDYRELLA while she tries to hold on to LAVINIA. It is done comically.)

CINDYRELLA. *(One arm held by each sister, her hat on backwards from the struggle.)* It's me, Lavender Sweet, your brother, Billy Sweet's daughter.

LAVINIA. *(Brushing herself off.)* My brother Billy's girl. What are you doing here? Where is your Daddy? Why didn't you call?

CINDYRELLA. My Dad passed. I — I've tried to call you on the telephone many times. But the line was always busy. *(Other two stare at PENELOPE who avoids their eyes.)*

LAVINIA. Well, what are you doing here? Why aren't you in some orphanage down South?

CINDYRELLA. *(Hangs head and takes letter from pocket. Hands letter to LAVINIA.)* Dad thought it best for me to be raised by my own kin. He says so in this letter.

LAVINIA. Ugh! Your hands are dirty.

CINDYRELLA. Sorry. *(Rubs hands on coat.)* I've been traveling for many hours.

LAVINIA. *(Opens the sealed letter while PENELOPE and ADRIENNE try to peek over her shoulder to see what it says.)* Don't I have enough mouths to feed? My unemployment is running out. I have to find a job. Now I have...What does this say *(Adjusts the letter, holding it close, then far away.)*

PENELOPE. *(Snatching the letter.)* Give it here, Momma, you know you can't read without your glasses. *(ADRIENNE hangs over PENELOPE who tries to move out of her line of vision.)* Dear Lavinia, Please take care of my only child. Under certain conditions, I want her raised by family...

LAVINIA. That's all right for him to say, but what about food, clothing...

ADRIENNE. *(Takes the letter from PENELOPE.)* I have instructed my lawyer to send you a monthly check from my investments...

LAVINIA. *(Snatching the letter.)* Give me that letter! *(She holds it at arms length.)* The money should prove s-s-, What is this big word?

CINDYRELLA. *(Standing with her head down in the distance.)*...sufficient.

LAVINIA. *(Gives CINDYRELLA a dirty look.)*...sufficient to take care of my daughter *(Her eyes grow wide and she pauses.)*...and your daughters. *(She drops the letter and holds her chest, smiling at her two daughters, daughters and mother hug each other and jump up and down.)*

CINDYRELLA. *(Picks up letter and holds it out.)* But, Aunt Lavinia, you didn't read the whole letter.

LAVINIA. *(Waving CINDYRELLA away.)* Just in the nick of time. *(Hugs daughters again.)*

CINDYRELLA. But...*(She lowers her head as if embarrassed and pockets the letter.)*

PENELOPE. Momma, you don't have to go to work.

ADRIENNE. You can stay home and bake cookies for us to eat after school.

LAVINIA. *(Separating herself from her daughters.)* Just put those want ads in the trash! *(Realizes that CINDYRELLA is still *standing with her head down, begins to weep crocodile tears.)* My poor brother, taken from us so soon! Girls, can't you shed a tear for your uncle, your rich uncle!

PENELOPE & ADRIENNE. *(Fake weeping.)* Poor Uncle Billy — gone too soon.

LAVINIA. *(Drying her fake tears.)* Now, my dear. *(She approaches CINDYRELLA.)* Your Daddy didn't give you a little something else to give to me, did he?

CINDYRELLA. Well, not exactly. *(Reaches into her pocket.)* He did give me some money...

LAVINIA. *(Snatching the money from CINDYRELLA.)* I'll just put this away for safe keeping. *(Smiling in a nasty way.)*

CINDYRELLA. ...for emergencies. *(She looks bewildered.)*

LAVINIA. Of course, our house is not as big as the one you came from. We work for a living. Let's see. Where can you sleep?

PENELOPE. Well, she can't sleep with us. We sleep in the living room with the TV.

ADRIENNE. You, of course, have the bed room, Momma. I guess she'll just have to sleep in the kitchen.

CINDYRELLA. The kitchen is fine. Really. Daddy always said that I could sleep any-where. I sometimes would sleep in the barn with my pony...

PENELOPE. You had a pony! *(She waddles over to CINDYRELLA and looks at her as if she were ready to punch her.)*

ADRIENNE. *(Swoops up the suitcase and puts it on the table.)* Let's see what you brought in here. *(She starts to open it.)*

CINDYRELLA. *(Rushes over to the table.)* Be careful...

LAVINIA. *(Taking CINDYRELLA by the arm.)* Don't worry. I'll see that you are dressed...the way you should be.

PENELOPE. *(Joining her sister at the suitcase.)* Just look at this stuff! *(She picks up a shirt.)* A Tommy Heflinger. *(She holds it in front of her.)*

ADRIENNE. This is my favorite color. *(She sneezes into it.)* Sorry. I'll just take it and...have it washed.

PENELOPE. These clothes are too — too —

LAVINIA. ...Big for you. You are so slender...

ADRIENNE. Yes, slender. You are a regular Slenderella!

PENELOPE. And, and, These clothes are too — too...

LAVINIA. Clean for you. Your hands are all sooty and — and cindery! *(CINDYRELLA looks at her hands and rubs them together.)*

PENELOPE. Cindyrella! Yes, that's a great name for you. *(She turns to her sister.)* May I introduce you to my Cousin, Cindyrella.

ADRIENNE. Did you say Cindyrella or Skinnyella? Ha-Ha.

LAVINIA. Girls, girls. Why don't you take that suitcase into my bedroom...for safe-keeping? You can leave that. *(Pointing to a picture of CINDYRELLA'S father.)* I will take very good care of you, never fear. *(Aunt and cousins exerunt.)*

CINDYRELLA. *(Looks at the picture of her father and sighs.)* Dad, I don't think that this *(Looks around the room and at the bedroom door.)* is what you had in mind. Dad, nothing is the same without you. *(Faces audience and sings...)*

I USE TO HAVE THE UPS.
NOW, I'VE GOT THE DOWNS. OH, NO.
I USE TO LIKE TO SMILE.
NOW, ALL I WANT TO DO IS FROWN.

DAD, IT'S NOT THE SAME WITHOUT YOU.
DAD, IT'S NOT THE SAME. WHAT HAD I OUGHT TO DO?

I THOUGHT I'D GIVE MY AUNT AND COUSINS ALL A
    GREAT BIG HUG.
I KNOW I SHOULDN'T OUGHT'A GIVE 'EM ALL A GREAT
    BIG SLUG.
IT'S MIGHTY, MIGHTY TEMPTING WHEN FOLKS BEGIN TO
    TREAT YOU WRONG
TO FORGET WHAT DAD TAUGHT YOU, TAUGHT YOU, ALL
    ALONG.
DAD, IT'S JUST NOT THE SAME WITHOUT YOU.
DAD, IT'S NOT THE SAME. HELP ME KNOW WHAT TO DO.

(Piano continues playing softly in the background. CINDYRELLA picks up the picture of her Father and hugs it. She puts it on the table, takes off her coat and hat, lays them on the floor in front of the stove. She rubs her eyes, lets out a little sigh. She lies down and curls into a fetal position.)

CURTAIN

Scene 2

(Same setting as above. PENELOPE and ADRIENNE are sitting at the table. CINDYRELLA is serving them breakfast. The sisters are wearing clothes that the audience recognizes as coming from CINDYRELLA's suitcase. CINDYRELLA has on the same clothes that she had on previously. They look a little shabbier.)

PENELOPE. Cindyrella, I'd like a little more syrup for my pancakes. You should know by now how much I like.

ADRIENNE. *(Sneezes and blows her nose loudly.)* Never mind all that syrup stuff. We have to get started on what we are going to do for the talent search. Imagine, Prince Records and Video Company is looking for talent right here in *(Local town/city.)* at the *(Local)* Center.

PENELOPE. It's a good thing Momma picked up those forms right away. Why can't we just put our name down and all that stuff when we get there? No, we have to get the forms before we get there. Momma should let us stay home from school today to work on our act.

ADRIENNE. What do you mean, our act? I'm going to dance. *(She gets up and begins dancing, then falls over her feet onto the couch.)*

PENELOPE. *(Laughing)* Oh, yea, your going to dance all right! I'm going to sing. *(She stands up and, off key sings.)*

ME-ME-ME-ME!

ADRIENNE. *(Putting her hands over her ears.)* You may be right, for once. We better work on our act.

LAVINIA. *(ENTERING from stage left.)* What is all of this racket? How am I going to get any beauty sleep? Cindyrella, where's my coffee? *(Sits down at the table. CINDYRELLA hands her a cup of coffee.)*

CINDYRELLA. Here you are, Auntie.

LAVINIA. Here you are, Auntie. Don't think that you are

going to soften me up. Here it is three days before the end of the month and no check has arrived from that fool lawyer your Daddy hired. If it doesn't come by Saturday, you are not going to be welcome here any longer.

ADRIENNE. That's right, Momma. You tell her. She forgot to do my math homework yesterday and the teacher made me stay after school. *(Crosses arms and pouts.)*

PENELOPE. Cindyrella, we have to get ready for the talent search. You have a lot to do. Don't forget. *(As intro to song begins on piano.)*, wash the floor; clean the yard; sweep the sidewalk...

(The three Krualls break into song and dance around as CINDYRELLA scurries about packing lunches, clearing the table and writing a list of the jobs told to her through the song.)

CINDYRELLA, CINDYRELLA, WASH THE FLOORS AND DO
    THE DISHES
CINDYRELLA, COME FRY THE FISHES.

CINDYRELLA CINDYRELLA, MAKE SOME COOKIES,
    RINSE OUR LAUNDRY,
CINDYRELLA, NEXT , CLEAN THE WINDOWS.
CINDYRELLA, CINDYRELLA, COMB OUR HAIR, AND DO
    OUR HOMEWORK,
CINDYRELLA WILL STAY FOREVER.
CINDYRELLA WILL STAY FOREVER. *(Ad lib)*

(The Krualls surround CINDYRELLA and repeat the last line. CINDYRELLA puts her hands over her ears.)

LAVINIA. *(Clapping her hands)* Now, girls, let's not over do it. Hurry or you'll be late for school.

PENELOPE & ADRIENNE. *(Kiss LAVINIA loudly on the cheek.)* 'By, Momma. See you later.

LAVINIA. Good-by, my precious ones. Don't let anybody hassle you. Remember, you're better than anybody! *(She similes until the door closes and then turns to CINDYRELLA.)* And don't start with that, "When am I...going to school?" stuff. I told you that you go to school when your records come.

CINDYRELLA. *(Bringing over the coffee pot and pouring more.)* Auntie, you can't register me for school if you don't send for the records.

LAVINIA. Register, register, register — all this paper work gives me a headache. *(Pauses, looking puzzled.)* They won't come...I knew that. I was waiting for you to realize that. It will teach you a lesson. Send for your school records after you clean the yard today.

CINDYRELLA. Yes, Auntie.

LAVINIA. I'm going shopping today. I want my girls to look really good for the talent search, so I'm going to buy them some new clothes. *(She stands up and sucks in her waist.)* Do you think I could pass for seventeen? It's not fair! *(EXIT stage right.)*

CURTAIN

Scene 3

(The stage is divided into three equal parts from front to back a fence, or hedge row separates each section to represent three adjacent back yards. The center yard is strewn with crumpled up paper. The other two yards are clean. When the curtain opens, CINDYRELLA is slowly picking up the paper in the center yard, and putting it into a trash bag that she is carrying. MR. GILL comes from stage left carrying a lawn chair.)

MR.GILL. *(Looks over fence after he has set up the chair.)* Good morning, Miss. Has grouchy Mrs. Kruall and her two nasty daughters finally moved from this neighborhood?

CINDYRELLA. *(Looking around her.)* Are you talking to me, Sir?

MR. GILL. I guess I am. Unless you see somebody that I don't.

CINDYRELLA. *(Giggling)* No, Sir. I guess I was just day-dreaming and didn't see you come out.

MR. GILL. My name is Jeremiah Gill. *(He reaches over the fence to shake hands.).* Cindyrella *(Reaches over to take MR. GILL's hand.)* They call me Cindyrella.

MR. GILL. *(Shaking CINDYRELLA's hand.)* Pleased to meet you Miss Cindyrella. I'm glad somebody is finally cleaning up that mess. Mrs. Kruall's been on unemployment for nearly a year and hasn't once picked up one little piece of paper. Of course, her daughters are just as lazy. Say, what are you doing here, anyway?

CINDYRELLA. I'm — I'm staying with my Aunt and Cousins, for a while. I — I just thought I'd make myself useful and — and help out a little.

MR. GILL. *(Laughing)* No offense to your relatives, but you sure picked the wrong ones to visit. They'll have you doing all the work. *(Chuckles)* Don't mind me. I'm just an old fashioned neighbor. I like neighbors who care about their yard and about each other. Now that one, pointing to the third yard, is a little strange, but she is a good neighbor.

CINDYRELLA. *(Looking at the third yard, then turning back to MR. GILL.)* Her yard looks nice. Even that little building in the back is painted a pretty shade of red. Why is she strange?

MR. GILL. When you see her, you will know what I mean. It is just that her ways are Island ways. She comes from some place in the Caribbean — keeps chickens, in that little building. Imagine, keeping chickens in the city-suburbs.

CINDYRELLA. I see. Well, it was nice to meet you, Mr. Gill. I had better get back to work.

MR. GILL. Here I am like an old man going on and on. This chair is for my nephew, Junior. He's going to sit out here for a few minutes to rest in the sun. He has a very high pressure job. He needs to rest before his really busy day. Good-by for now, Miss Cindyrella. *(EXITS)*

CINDYRELLA. Good-by, Mr. Gill.

(She stretches and lifts her face to the sun. she cocks her head to listen to bird calls from off stage; she takes a big gulp of air and hugs herself smiling. JUNIOR ENTERS from stage left, doesn't notice her, but sits in the lawn chair. He is wearing sun glasses and shorts; he relaxes in the chair and looks up at the sun overhead. CINDYRELLA begins to sing.)

CINDYRELLA.
OLD MOTHER NATURE'S IN A GOOD MOOD TODAY.
ALL HER LITTLE SONG-BIRDS HAVE COME OUT TO PLAY.
(Chorus)

THEY TWITTER; THEY CHIRP; THEY WARBLE; THEY SING.
THEY COCK THEIR TINY HEADS AND LIFT THEIR
    GRACEFUL WING. *(Chorus)*

THEIR COLORS DOT THE GRASS. THEY SIT UP IN THE
    TREES.
THEY SING THEIR PRETTY SONG, THEN FLY OFF IN THE
    BREEZE. *(Chorus)*

(She pauses, then picks up her trash bag and continues working. While she is singing, JUNIOR gets up from his chair and watches her from the other side of the fence. When she stops singing, he claps. She jumps, startled.)

JUNIOR. *(CHARMING)*. Very nice, Miss. It seems as if the birds in this yard aren't the only ones to sing.

CINDYRELLA. I apologize for disturbing you, Sir. Mr. Gill said that you needed to rest. You have an important job that keeps you very busy.

JUNIOR. I always have time to listen to a pretty song. I hope that you are going to sing for the talent search at the *(Local center.)* on Saturday.

CINDYRELLA. Goodness, no. I can't.

JUNIOR. Why not? You live in *(Local town/city.)*. You are between twelve and seventeen. You can sing! What else is there?

CINDYRELLA. Well, ah, well, ah, you need to get a registration form before the audition.

JUNIOR. *(Laughing)* Is that all? *(Reaches into his pocket and pulls out a form.)* Here. *(He hands the form over the fence.)* Now you have a form. *(She takes the form.)*

MR. GILL. *(From off stage.)* Junior, Junior, telephone. It sounds important.

JUNIOR. *(Hurrying off stage left.)* No excuses! Show up for the talent search.

CINDYRELLA. *(Shouting)* Thank you! *(Looks down at the form and then holds it to her heart.)* Wouldn't it be wonderful to audition. Maybe Aunt Lavinia will let me go...*(Interrupted by a noise in the next yard)*.

MRS. ZEBALON. *(Off stage.)* Here, chick, chick *(Repeat)*.

(Backing on stage from stage right comes Mrs. Zebalon; wearing a brightly colored head-wrap and a long skirt with an apron that has pockets; smoking a corn-cob pipe and carrying a basket of eggs.) That ought to hold them a while. *(Turns and sees CINDYRELLA watching her.)* Those chickens eat more than three dogs. But, a dog can't give you these. *(She holds up the basket of eggs.)* Come on over here, Missy, and feel these eggs. They're still warm. Ain't noth'en will bring you better luck than touching warm chicken eggs. *(CINDYRELLA hesitates.)* Come on, now. Ain't noth'en gonna hurt you.

CINDYRELLA. *(Slowly reaching over the fence, touches the eggs, smiles.)* Since my Dad left me, life keeps changing me. I can't seem to change life. Do you know what I mean?

ZEBALON. Well, yes and no. People make changes for themselves and others all the time. Look at that yard. When you came out here this morning, it looked like a hurricane went through it. But, you changed all that. *(CINDYRELLA looks toward the yard.)* See. *(CINDYRELLA turns toward MRS. ZEBALON, her eyes widening.)* I told you. Don't you feel better?

CINDYRELLA. (Pulling her hand away fast.) Who said I felt bad? How do you know how I feel?

ZEBALON. Oh, I know a lot of things. I know you been live'n in that house with those Krualls for nearly a month now. I know you a relative and I know somebody else raised you up.

CINDYRELLA. *(Mouth open, hands on hips.)* How do you know all of that! I never met you before.

ZEBALON. Just cause I ain't a nosy neighbor don't mean I ain't a know'en neighbor. I know you can sing, too.

CINDYRELLA. Do you really think so? Mr. Gill's nephew seems to think the same thing. He gave me this registration form for the talent search on Saturday. It's — it's too bad that I can't go.

ZEBALON. Who says you can't go?

CINDYRELLA. I just don't really think that my Aunt will take me. I wish...

ZEBALON. Yes, you wish — what do you wish?

CINDYRELLA. *(Puffing up the trash bag.)* What difference does it make what I wish.

ZEBALON. Change happens.When you came out here this morning, that yard was a mess, you didn't have no registration form for no audition, but now you do. Besides, now you know me!

  CINDYRELLA. I guess that's all true. *(Smiling)* Ma'am, you do make me almost believe in the impossible.

  ZEBELON. Now you're talk'en.

  CINDYRELLA. Do — do you think that you...no. It's too much to ask.

  ZEBALON. No, it ain't. You wan'na ask me to help you get to the audition. Well, I'm gon'na do that, and a whole lot more. What are good neighbors for?

(Rap beat)
GOOD NEIGHBORS ARE BETTER THAN
CHAINS AND CHAINS OF GOLD
IT REALLY DOESN'T MATTER IF THEY'RE YOUNG OR IF
THEY'RE OLD. *(Chorus)*

THEY'RE CLOSE TO YOU AS FAMILY BECAUSE THEY LIVE
RIGHT NEXT DOOR.
THEY'RE ALWAYS RICH IN SOMETHING.
DON'T CHALK'EM
OFF AS POOR. *(Chorus)*

SOMETIMES THEY WATCH THE BABY
WHEN MOMMA GOES TO WORK.

THEY CALL THE FOLKS AT 911
WHEN NASTY PEOPLE LURK. *(Chorus)*

GOOD NEIGHBORS MIND THEIR BUSINESS, BUT
ALWAYS
LEND A HAND
TO TAKE IN BAGS OF GROCERIES,
PLAY IN YOUR COUSIN'S BAND. *(Chorus)*

  ZEBALON. On Saturday, after your Aunt and her two uglies have gone, you come over to my house. I will have everything ready that you will need. In the mean time, *(She reaches into her pocket and takes out a chicken foot.)* you sleep with this under your pillow every night. While you be sleep'en, it will scratch away all the things that will stop you from winning the talent search.

CINDYRELLA. *(Reluctantly takes the foot.)* Where is the rest of the chicken, if you don't mind my asking?

ZEBALON. No, I don't mind. That chicken's where all the rest of my dead chickens is. Right here! *(She points to and rubs her belly.)* And, that one was real good, so his foot should work real well. See you Saturday morning. *(EXIT)*

CINDYRELLA. *(Shrugs, puts the foot into her pocket.)* What have I got to lose? *(Shrugs and finishes picking up papers as curtain closes.).*

CURTAIN

Scene 4

(The living room/kitchen of the Kruall house. The two girls are looking off to stage far right. It appears to the audience that they are looking into a mirror. They keep fussing with their hair, trying this and that bow, fussing with their clothes which are suppose to be fancy, but are really rather silly. LAVINIA is on the telephone and CINDYRELLA is at an ironing board in the kitchen area, ironing. Her clothes are the same that she has been wearing. They are more shabby than ever.)

LAVINIA. What did you say? *(Pause)* The check is in the mail? I heard that one before. In fact, I said that one before. *(Pause)* But, you mean it. Well, Mr. hot-shot lawyer, if that check does not get here before the end of the day little Miss Goodie Two-Shoes will not be welcome to live with her next of kin. *(Pause)* By 12:30 p.m. today? Yes, someone will be here to receive it by certified mail. Good-by. *(Turns to CINDYRELLA.)* Did you here that,Cindyrella? That check is going to be here by certified mail today. You make sure that you are standing by this door waiting for it. The girls and I have to be at the *(Local)* Center. I just know that one of them will win first prize. Then we can all, well, almost all of us can move to California, the home of the stars.

PENELOPE. Momma, which bow do you like better? I just can't make up my mind.

ADRIENNE. That is if you had a mind to make up! *(Sneezes and blows nose.)*

PENELOPE. Momma, did you hear that? It would serve her right to sneeze right in the middle of our beautiful skit. Then everyone would know that I'm the real star in the family.

ADRIENNE. You wish upon a star. That's the closest you'll ever get.

LAVINIA. Girls, girls. You must hurry and get ready. Cindyrella, bring those pressed jackets over here. And, oh, yes, find that tape of they're act. I'm sure the talent scouts will want to review it over and over, after they've seen my girls live. *(Everyone hustles around with a great show of getting ready.)*

CINDYRELLA. Here it is, Aunt Lavinia. Do you have your registration forms? *(The girls hold them up.)* How about your tape? *(The girls holds it up.)* The front door key? *(LAVINIA holds it up.)* Does anyone have to go to the bathroom?

LAVINIA. Really, Cindyrella, I'm the Mother around here. Does anyone have to go to the bathroom?

PENELOPE & ADRIENNE. No, Momma. Let's go!

(The three nearly trip over one and other heading for the door — stage right. LAVINIA stops everyone and looks at CINDYRELLA.)

LAVINIA. Cindyrella, aren't you going to wish your cousins luck?

CINDYRELLA. *(Putting her hands behind her back broadly, so that the audience can see, crosses fingers on both hands.)* Good luck, Penelope. Good luck, Adrienne. *(All exit, but CINDYRELLA. She stands on tip-toes craning her neck to make sure that they are gone. Turning toward the audience.)* Let's see. I have my registration form. *(She pulls it out of her pocket.)* I have to be back here by 12:30P.M. I've slept with the chicken foot under my pillow, well, my hat — same thing. Mrs. Zebalon, you are a strange one, but you've been a good neighbor to me. I hope that you are ready for me. *(EXIT)*

CURTAIN

ACT II

Scene I

(The stage is dim. In the center of the stage is a large trunk or box. Scattered around are large baskets. Bright colored cloth or flowers spill out of the baskets. It is a room in MRS. ZEBALON's house. Electric candles may add to the mystery of the place. MRS. ZEBALON is humming to herself while arranging things inside the big box.)

CINDYRELLA. *(ENTERS stage right.)* Hello, anybody home? *(On tip toe and wearing her hat and her coat. She partially hides her face, as if she is embarassed).*

ZEBALON. Come in, child. Come in. I am already for you. Look what I have for your outward transformation? *(Holds up a distinctive wig and a brightly colored outfit.)* Take these and go over there and put them on *(Points to stage left.)*

CINDYRELLA. *(Pleased, takes the wig and costume.)* Oh, thank you, Mrs. Zebalon. *(She skips off stage left.)*

ZEBALON. *(Smiling and shaking her head, picks up telephone and dials.)* Hello, Johnny Boy? She's here. Come and pick her up. *(Pause)* What? What do you mean if she is not finished by the stroke of noon you will leave her there? Johnny Boy, don't be a rat. Your boss will not fire you, if you are late. *(Pause)* I have plenty of chicken feet, but you must get here fast.

CINDYRELLA. *(ENTERS stage left with head down dragging herself.)* This is a beautiful outfit. But, I don't know. The registration form says that each contestant should bring a tape of his or her act. I don't have a tape. I don't even know where the *(Local Center)* is. And I have to be home by 12:30 P.M. to...

ZEBALON. *(Looking at her carefully.)* The outer transformation looks pretty good. Now I need to work on the inner transformation. Cindyrella, have I been a good neighbor to you?

CINDYRELLA. You've been the best neighbor.

ZEBALON. Have I let you down yet?

CINDYRELLA. No, but...

ZEBALON. No buts about it. You just have to trust me a little longer. Close your eyes. Not too tight. *(CINDYRELLA closes her eyes.)* I just have to remember the words for the inner transformation. Obi - obi - humm oma - oma - humm - *(Takes a step toward the audience and looks out over it.)* what is that last part? *(Pause)* Udo! *(Sings Obi Oma Udo! and moves in rhythm to the background drum patterns being played off stage, or in front of the stage. Repeat the words and rhythms. Use moving spots, a chorus and/or dancers, if desired.).* Obi oma udo. means, Peace, Good Heart in lbo, a tribal language spoken in Nigeria.

CINDYRELLA. *(Head shoots up and lights come up at the same time, on final oma. smile on face, eyes flashing.)* Where's the phone book. I'll find that place, tape or no tape. Mr. Charming of Prince Records will hear my voice. I'll be back to get that check too. Just see if that old Aunt of mine gets her hands on it!

ZEBALON. Oh, I did a real good job. I can see that. *(Sound of motor cycle and knock on door.)* That'll be my nephew, Johnny Boy Raton. He is going to take you to the Center and he will bring you home. *(She reaches into the trunk.)* Here is a tape recorder. I'll ask him to wait outside for a few minutes while you make a tape. You've come so far. Let's just make sure that you have everything that you need. *(Louder knocking.)* Keep your shirt on, Johnny Boy. She's coming. *(EXITS right.)*

CINDYRELLA. I can't believe that this is happening. It is like a dream. *(EXITS left with tape recorder in her hand.)*

ZEBALON. *(ENTERING)* Johnny Boy is here, but he says that he must pick you up to take you home on the stroke of noon. He says that his boss will fire him if he is late. Besides, didn't you say you must be home to get a check or something...

(CINDYRELLA. Off stage she begins singing the song that she sang in the garden.)

CURTAIN

Scene 2

(The stage is clear, except for a microphone at the far left. At the far right apron, three chairs are set up. MR. CHARMING [Junior] and his two assistants are sitting there. A line of six auditioners stand off stage left. The KRUALLS are fourth; CINDYRELLA is sixth. This scene is really an opportunity for three acts to go on, as if in an audition. Assistants I and II ad lib as they introduce the acts.
ARSINO CHARMING [Junior] and assistants ad lib as they usher the acts on and off the stage. Samples below:
ASST. I. The next act will be ___________________
ASST. II. Thank you. That will be all.
CHARMING. Don't you call us. We'll call you.
Each performer hands one of the assistants a registration form and a tape. Each act should last no longer than one and one-half minutes. The acts, whether good or bad might end in an amus-ing manner. E.g., a dancer who wraps him/herself into the stage curtain in a final run; a trumpeter who holds his music up-side down through half of the piece; a dramatic reader who gets so into the reading that he/she runs off stage crying before the end; etc. Everything should move fast. The KRUALLS can ad lib by making faces at the performers, or other silly stuff, as long as it adds to the show. They should not distract the audi-ence from the performers. As the KRUALLS are called to the microphone, the audience sees CINDYRELLA carrying her registration form and her tape. She remains behind the fifth performer.)

ASST. I. *(Addressing the KRUALLS.)* All right, ladies, you are on. Do your best!

ASST. II. Action!

PENOLOPE. A Drama, by Penelope and Adrienne Kruell. *(Clears her throat and addresses ADRIENNE.)* You like Tyrone from music class. Don't you?

ADRIENNE. No, I don't.

PENELOPE. Yes, you do.
ADRIENNE. No, I don't!
PENELOPE. Yes, you do!
ADRIENNE. N-N-N- *(Puts finger under nose to prevent sneeze. Sways around the stage continuing the "n" sound. PENELOPE is jumping up and down waving her fists.).* Ach—o-o-o!
CHARMING. Cut. That's it ladies. Thank you for coming. Did you leave your tape with my assistant? Next, please.
PEN. & ADR. *(Girls cling to microphone.)* Please, give us another chance. We can do better.

(ASSISTANTS I and II move to help the girls off the stage. Girls make pleading noises and motions as they are escorted off.)

CHARMING. *(Noticing CINDYRELLA, leaves his seat and goes over to her as the fifth contestant approaches the microphone.)* Don't I know you? You look familiar.
CINDYRELLA. *(Recognizing JUNIOR, smiles as the clock off stage begins to chime.)* Ah - ah, no comprendo.
CHARMING. *(Returning to his seat looking puzzled.)* It's those eyes. I've seen them somewhere...

(ASSISTANT II Introduces the next act, ad libs. The clock keeps chiming. Charming keeps looking at CINDYRELLA. Contestant keeps raising and lowering the microphone, scratching his/her head, clearing his/her throat, etc. When the clock reaches the tenth stroke, CINDYRELLA drops her tape and registration form and runs off stage.)

CHARMING. Wait, wait. *(Runs after CINDYRELLA off stage. Audience hears motorcycle pull away.)*
ASST. I. *(Picking up tape and form and putting them on CHARMING's chair.)* I think the boss will want to look at this.

CURTAIN

Scene 3

*(Kruall's apartment. The rooms are all neat and tidy. CINDYRELLA
is sitting on a straight chair wearing her old hat and coat. She
has two pieces of paper in her hand. One is her father's letter;
the other looks like a check. The KRUALLS ENTER stage
right.)*

PENELOPE.   And then Adrienne sneezed and those nasty
people wouldn't let us do it one more time! They were so mean!
  ADRIENNE. I was really good too. I was into it. No, I don't!!!
  LAVINIA. Girls, you did leave your tape, didn't you?
  PENELOPE & ADRIENNE. Yes, Momma we did!
  LAVINIA. That's it then. We'll give them until four o'clock,
then we'll call them.
  ADRIENNE. But, they kept saying, "Don't you call us. We'll
call you." *(Phone rings. All three dive for it. LAVINIA gets it.)*
  LAVINIA. *(Sweetly)* Hello, Kruall residence. *(Pause)* Yes,
yes I had a daughter who tried out for the talent search this morn-
ing. In fact, I had two daughters...*(The girls are dancing around,
each pointing to herself pantomiming, It's me.)*. Sing? My girls can
do anything. If you want them to sing, they'll sing. You're what?
(Pause) You're calling from a cell phone — right outside the house.
Why of course you can come in!

*(Hangs up. The girls and LAVINIA stand in front of the mirror,
    pushing each other to get space, fixing their hair, etc. ad lib-
    bing. Knock at door.)*

THE KRULLES. Answer the door, Cindyrella.

*(Mother and daughters sit and smile as CHARMING and his Uncle,
    MR. GIBBS enter. CINDYRELLA keeps her face turned away.)*

LAVINIA. *(Rising from her chair, extends her hand to
CHARMING.)* Hello, Mr. Charming. Welcome to our happy home.
(In a nasty voice.) Gibbs, what are you doing here, trying to jinx us!
  MR. GIBBS. No, Lavinia. You can do that yourself. *(She gives
him a dirty look, and then smiles at CHARMING.)*

LAVINIA. Won't you sit down, Mr. Charming.

CHARMING. No, thank you. I just have time to hear your daughter sing *(Holds up CINDYRELLA's tape.)* and then we must be off to Hollywood.

PENELOPE. *(Jumps up.)* Me first. I'm the oldest!

LAVINIA. Yes, darling. Stand up nice and tall and let Mr. Charming hear you.

PENELOPE. Any appropriate song? (*Sings in a high squeaky voice. Everyone looks at each other. MR. GIBBS covers his ears.)*

CHARMING. Thank you, Miss Kruall. That will do. May I hear your sister.

PENELOPE. But, Momma, that wasn't fair! *(Sits down angrily.)*

ADRIENNE. *(Sniffles, then sings one note and wavers as she tries to stifle a sneeze.)* A-A-Acho-o-o!!!

CHARMING. That isn't quite what we were looking for. Don't you have another daughter, Mrs. Kruall? *(Walks over to CINDYRELLA, takes both of her hands and helps her to stand up.)*

LAVINIA. Well, well, she, she is like a daughter...but she wasn't at the auditions today!

CHARMING. I wouldn't be too sure of that. Won't you please sing for us, Cindyrella?

PENELOPE. How does he know her name? *(Knock at door. She stamps over to it and opens it. ENTER ZEBALON. She has a kerchief full of things tied on a stick slung over her shoulder.)* What do you want?

ZEBALON. Hello, Penelope. I see you are your usual self today.

MR. GIBBS. Mrs. Zebalon, join the party. Cindyrella is about to sing.

LAVINIA. What is going on here?

MR. GIBBS. Just a few neighbors helping another neighbor.

(CINDYRELLA takes off her coat and hat and sings the song that she sang in the garden.)

CHARMING. *(Leading the clapping.)* I guess we have ourselves a winner. Mrs. Kruall, are you this child's guardian?

LAVINIA. I guess I am. *(Puffs out her chest.)*

CHARMING. Can you have your family packed up by four

o'clock this afternoon?

LAVINIA. Most certainly. Girls, girls, get your things together. Not you, Cindyrella. You talk to Mr. Charming.

CINDYRELLA. Just a minute, Aunt Lavinia. Do you recognize this? *(Holds up Father's letter.)*

LAVINIA. Of course, dear. That is your dear Father's letter to me.

CINDYRELLA. And it says, near the bottom. "If my Sister, Lavinia does not register as the legal guardian of my daughter in one month, all of the above is null and void."

LAVINIA. *(Snatching the letter and holding it out to read.)* Oh, no. There's that word again, *(Moves letter closer.)* REGISTER! It's in the fine print!

PENELOPE. Does that mean we can't go to Hollywood?

LAVINIA. No, precious. We are your cousin's only kin. She can't go alone.

CINDYRELLA. No, I won't go alone. But, Aunt Lavinia, you and my cousins are not coming with me. Neither are you getting this. *(Away and holds up check — ADRIENNA dives for it, but CINDYRELLA pulls it away and tears it up.).*

LAVINIA. You — you mean I'll have to get a job, a j-o-b!

PENELOPE. There won't be any pancakes for breakfast...

ADRIENNE. And nobody to do my math homework...W-a-a- *(Crying, joined by sister and mother.)*

CINDYRELLA. Thank you, Mr. Gibbs for your kindness. Mrs. Zebalon, I see that you are all packed. Would you please be a good neighbor and accompany me to Hollywood?

(She takes her by the arm. The whole cast comes on stage and sings and dances to the neighbor song. To the front right of the stage, the KRUALLS and MR. GIBBS pantamine talking to each other. At first hostile, as the song progresses, they smile at each other and shake hands, then join in the song.)

END OF PLAY

PROPERTIES

Act I - Scene 1, Scene 2, Scene 4 and Act II - Scene 3
Couch
Telephone on telephone table or cell phone
Stuffed chair
Three kitchen chairs
Kitchen table dishes and silver
Coffee pot
Stove refrigerator
Ironing board and iron
Suitcase containing clothes to be worn in Scene 2
Letter from Billy Sweet
Registration forms

Act I - Scene 3
Two fence posts
Optional, two fences
Lawn chair
Basket with few eggs inside
Litter (cans, papers, etc.)
Trash bag
Registration form

Act II – Scene 1
Large trunk
Tape recorder and tape
Three large baskets (or boxes) with flowers and/or bright colored
cloth spilling out
Optional, electric candles
Sound effect - motor cycle engine from offstage

Scene 2
Microphone Three chairs Sound effect - clock striking twelve off
stage

Scene 3
As listed above
Hobo pack on stick

COSTUMES

Cindyrella
Act I, scenes 1,2,3,4 - casual contemporary clothes, including hat
and coat
Act II, scene 1, same as above until change - wig; bright, dressy
clothes
Act II, scene 3, hat and coat over bright, dressy clothes

Adrienne
Contemporary clothes through-out except Act I, scene 2; clothes
from suitcase seen in Act I, scene 1; Act 1, scene 4 gaudy dress
with hair bows

Lavinia
Contemporary adult clothes through-out one change, optional

Arsinio Charming
Act I, scene 3, short sleeve shirt and shorts; all other scenes in
contemporary casual

Mr. Gill
Contemporary casual

Mrs. Zebalon
Long bright skirt and head kerchief through-out, shawl and corn cob
pipe, optional

All others
Contemporary casual through-out